KU-198-084

Can Dad Dance?

ACC. No: 07069211

'Can Dad Dance?'
An original concept by Steve Howson
© Steve Howson

Illustrated by Ellie Oshea

Published by MAVERICK ARTS PUBLISHING LTD

Studio 11, City Business Centre, 6 Brighton Road,

Horsham, West Sussex, RH13 5BB

© Maverick Arts Publishing Limited August 2020

+44 (0)1403 256941

A CIP catalogue record for this book is available at the British Library.

ISBN 978-1-84886-685-0

www.maverickbooks.co.uk

This book is rated as: Green Band (Guided Reading)
This story is mostly decodable at Letters and Sounds Phase 5.
Up to five non-decodable story words are included.

Can Dad Dance?

by Steve Howson

illustrated by
Ellie Oshea

Dad thinks he can win

the talent show.

TALENT SHOW

He says he can dance.

But I am not so sure...

He said he could bake,

but he messed up the mix.

POP!

He said he could slide,
but his bottom got stuck.

SQUEEZE!

He said he could fly,

but his wings let him down.

He said he had style,

but his clothes were alarming.

SWISH!

When we needed some shelves,
he said, "I can do it myself."

He said he could dive,

but he bounced far too high.

WHOOSH!

He said he could row,

but the boat would not go.

He said he was quick,

but he ended up last.

SLIDE!

So, do I think he can dance?

Oh no, I do not!

Dad jumped on the stage.

His costume sparkled.

His belly wobbled.

I hardly dared to look.

He gave me a wink and then he went...

POP!

SQUEEZE!

20

KRUMP!

SWISH!

21

23

I'd never seen a dance like that.

The crowd went wild,
they whooped and cheered.
The judges stood and clapped.

I could not believe my eyes.

That did not look like Dad to me.

Then Dad went up to claim his prize...

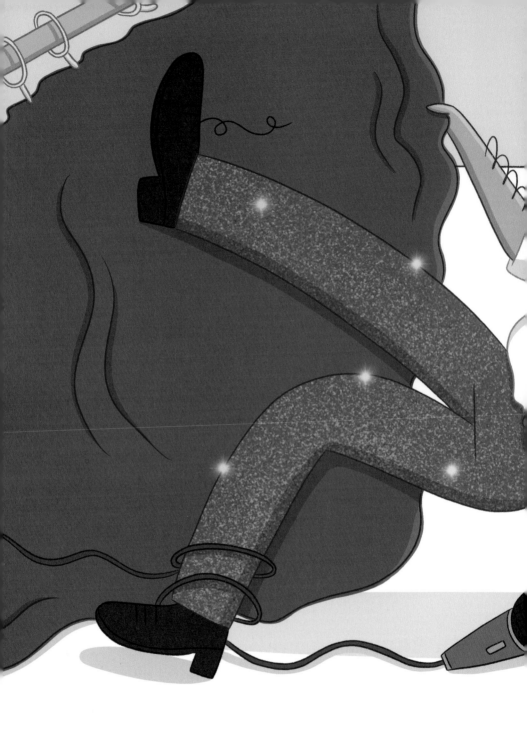

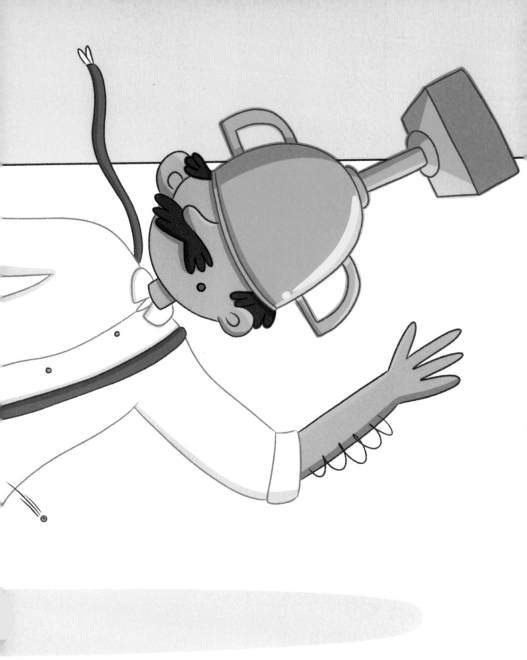

Now, that's more like the Dad I know!

Quiz

1. Dad thinks he can win the...
a) Party
b) Talent show
c) Disco

2. What sound did Dad make when he bounced too high?
a) Whoosh!
b) Zing!
c) Swish!

3. What sound did Dad make when he said he was quick but ended up last?
a) Crunch!
b) Flop!
c) Slide!

4. What did the judges do?

a) They stood and clapped

b) They frowned and shouted

c) They stood and booed

5. What did Dad do at the end?

a) He sang

b) He fell asleep

c) He tripped

Turn over for answers

Book Bands for Guided Reading

The Institute of Education book banding system is a scale of colours that reflects the various levels of reading difficulty. The bands are assigned by taking into account the content, the language style, the layout and phonics. Word, phrase and sentence level work is also taken into consideration.

Maverick Early Readers are a bright, attractive range of books covering the pink to white bands. All of these books have been book banded for guided reading to the industry standard and edited by a leading educational consultant.

Pink
Red
Yellow
Blue
Green
Orange
Turquoise
Purple
Gold
White

To view the whole Maverick Readers scheme, visit our website at
www.maverickearlyreaders.com

Or scan the QR code above to view our scheme instantly!

Quiz Answers: 1b, 2a, 3c, 4a, 5c